Blood Sacrifice

Published by

Two Realms Publishing LLC

https://tworealmspublishingllc.com

ISBN: 978-1-955106-45-0

Book Cover: RJ Creatives Graphic Services

Interior Design: Two Realms Publishing LLC

Editor: Ink It Out Editing

1st edition 2025

Author's Note

This is kind of a warning, but not the kind you're thinking of.

Or that I normally give.

If you're like me and you enjoy a chronological reading order, then here it is.

Be forewarned, you will have to jump to another series and well, things get brutal and dirty (the good kind, as well as the bad) in there. They might get a little bloody here, too.

Blood Sacrifice
Hunted
Rebel Tides (Prisma Isle™ 3)
Siren's Curse (Prisma Isle™ 4)
Silencing the Shape Shifter (Prisma Isle™ 5)
Kingdom of Embers (Prisma Isle™ 6)

Then back to this series.

Blood Sacrifice

THE ATLIS CHRONICLES

A PRISMA ISLE™ SERIES SPIN-OFF

PREQUEL

KRYS FENNER

TWO REALMS PUBLISHING LLC

The Attis Chronicles

Blood Sacrifice

Prisma Isle™

Perfectly Reckless

Chaotic Tranquility

Rebel Tides

One

Thalasia tucked a loose strand of her oxford blue hair behind her ear as she glanced over her shoulder. That dark-haired man was still behind her. Was he following her, or was it just a coincidence? He'd appeared on the wooded trail behind her on the other side of the market, and hadn't turned off anywhere since she'd gotten here. But that didn't mean he was after her or the object in her possession. No one knew what she'd retrieved for the shaman. Hell, she didn't even know. It looked like a golden scroll with a bunch of gibberish, or at least a lot of symbols she didn't understand. Not that it mattered. Especially if she wanted to get paid.

And she needed the money.

Which meant she had to lose this guy. Better to be on the safe side. Besides, this was the human world, it was best she didn't draw any attention to herself. Though she kind of itched for a fight. Maybe if she got somewhere secluded...then she could *really* handle the situation.

Scanning the street, she searched over the open stores and various vendors. There were a couple of people selling fruit and other produce, a few with fish stalls, and a guy wheeling a barrel of flowers from a nearby alley. That was her escape route. It wasn't private by any means, but it would work.

Quickening her pace, Thalasia darted in and out of the crowd. She peered back over her shoulder just as the dark-haired male strode a little faster through the throng of people. Her heart thundered beneath her chest. *Shit!* She couldn't go invisible yet and with the number of humans around, fighting wasn't the best option. It left her with only one other choice.

Letting out a low whistle, she conjured up a small gust of wind. Nothing out of the ordinary, just enough to knock over a few pieces of fish. She glimpsed the male; his attention fell to the situation as the owner ran into the road and cleaned up the mess. Thalasia ducked down and crawled around to the back of the closest stall, startling a blue-eyed male on the other side. She pressed a finger to her lips and silently mouthed, "Please."

Goddess, she couldn't do anything to manipulate the human. Not without giving away her position. She prayed this guy didn't say anything. *Please, Demeter. Let this work.*

With a slight dip of his chin, the male flashed a toothy smile at the next customer who approached. "How can I help you?"

Thank the goddess for small favors, Thalasia thought to herself. She'd wait out her hunter. Hopefully, it wouldn't take long for him to get far enough away that she could leave. She'd glamour if she could, blend in with the stall, but magic like that would cause a scene. And there was no telling if the person chasing her possessed his own kind of power. He could be human for all she knew.

Not that it would make much sense. The shaman who'd contracted her to hunt this scroll down had known she wasn't human. While he hadn't guessed everything, he'd figured out enough. Now, she just had to get back to his shop. In one piece.

"Thank you. Come again," the blue-eyed man replied as he held out a white package.

"Excuse me," a male said. "My niece got away from me and I'm just trying to find her. Have you seen a young girl with blue hair run past here?"

Thalasia stiffened, pressing her back more against the stall. Her eyes widened a touch. Fuck. This guy really had followed her. Who the fuck was he?

"No, sorry. Can't say that I have."

"Are you sure? She's about...yay tall and has bright silver eyes."

"I'm certain." Her savior grinned. "Now, excuse me, but I have a customer." His attention shifted to another person, and he uttered something in a foreign language.

Although she'd spent most of the last year in the human world, she hadn't learned any of their tongues. The ones she knew weren't of this world. Thalasia flicked her gaze as someone huffed and walked away from the stall. It sounded like her stalker, but she didn't budge. Tucking her knees against her chest, she listened in on her savior's exchange. Not that she understood a single word, but it was better to focus on him than her erratic heartbeat. Or how her lungs constricted inside her chest. Fuck. What if *he* hadn't left? What if he hung around and waited?

The blue-eyed stranger bent down and retrieved two sheets of white paper. "I still see him, so stay put," he whispered. The male straightened, filled the sheets with three pieces of fish, and concluded his transaction.

Thalasia nodded and blew out a silent sigh of relief. Gods, she could breathe. While she wasn't safe yet, at least this guy had helped her out. Which meant freedom couldn't be too far around the corner. She'd get the scroll to the shaman, collect her fee, and leave this town. As much as she liked Japan, it might be time to jump to another realm and leave the human world behind.

Her rescuer crouched down on his haunches and dug around in a cabinet. "Do you know this man?"

"No," she replied, keeping her voice low. Though the surrounding din likely covered their exchange, she refused to chance it.

"Where are your parents?"

"I'm alone," Thalasia muttered. It was the last thing she wished to admit, but it was the truth. Not that she wanted to think about that, or how it had all happened.

"Oh...well, um, I'm Bayani and I'll keep you safe. Just..." his words trailed off as he lifted his gaze and surveyed the market. "I don't see him, but wait a little longer. Okay?"

"Yeah," she mumbled.

With a dip of his chin, he rose to his feet and returned to his task. She paid it little attention. Yeah, she was a twelve-year-old out in the world on her own, but so what? She wouldn't feel sorry for herself. Things had happened and no one could change them. All she could do now was focus on her survival. That was what mattered the most.

Thalasia pressed her shoulder against the heavy oak door and gave it a good shove. It opened with a slight hiss as the bell above it rang. Her eyebrows furrowed as she flicked her gaze from the door to the store itself. She didn't recall it taking so much effort the first time. A chill swept down her spine. Shaking the sensation off, Thalasia shut the door. The bell sounded again, ringing loudly in her ears. Ensuring there were no interruptions while she conducted the last of their business, she locked the door and flipped the sign.

Whether the shaman knew it, he was temporarily closed. Thalasia surveyed the store, glossing over the various earmarked books, herbs, and other miscellaneous items. "Ayumu," she called out as she stepped farther into the shop. Although she didn't see him, the magician had to be around somewhere. Or maybe he was a warlock. She wasn't positive.

"I see you have returned safely, Miss Thalasia."

"Fuck!" She jumped back and eyed the dark-skinned, bald-headed magic wielder. Where the fuck had he just come from? Because he sure as shit wasn't there a second ago.

"Such colorful language in such a young girl." He clasped his hands behind him and strolled toward the counter.

"I don't recall my age being an issue when you sent me on that quest," she retorted as she trailed behind him. It shouldn't matter at all, really, though someone always had some kind of comment about it. So what if she was a kid? She got things done.

"Does this mean you have retrieved the scroll?"

His response and lack of valid concern didn't surprise her. Dragging her fingers through her blue locks, she dropped a hand to her hip, swallowed the groan on the tip of her tongue, and let out an exasperated sigh. "Yeah.

And you should pay me extra. Apparently, you weren't the only one after it."

"Oh?" He cocked a dark eyebrow at her. "Did you have difficulty obtaining it?"

"No. But I had someone following me through the market. And he got pretty close." And if it hadn't been for Bayani, he might have caught her. Not that she mentioned that. It didn't seem all that important. Plus, she didn't want anything to come back on her rescuer.

"As you obviously escaped him, it seems you are worth your fare." One corner of his mouth quirked up. Ayumu stepped around the counter and his golden eyes focused on her. "Now come, show me the scroll."

"Money first." She'd learned the hard way to see payment before she handed over the item in question. One person had the audacity to run off with said treasure. He hadn't gotten far, but she hated having to hurt the guy. As she didn't know what kind of magic this male possessed, it was better if she avoided a fight.

Ayumu balled up his fist and then opened up his hand. A small blue pouch rested against the ball of his large palm. "Your turn, Miss Thalasia."

Yep, definitely a sorcerer. While she had her own magic that she could've hidden the scroll in, simple worked best. Thalasia untied the purple velvet pouch she had attached to the belt loop of her jeans. It didn't look like anything other than a small purse. An extension charm worked wonders on something so common. She dug into it, retrieved the golden case he'd sent her to find, and held it out. "As promised."

"Set it on the counter and you may collect your fee."

She raised an eyebrow at him. Why wouldn't he just take it from her hand? Whatever. He was paying her, so it didn't matter if he was a little eccentric. She placed the kaleidoscope-sized case on the counter, picked up the blue pouch, and checked it to verify he'd filled it. The pouch contained a multitude of beautiful gold coins, along with a couple rubies and emeralds. She grinned. "It was a pleasure doing business with you."

"Yes, it was," he replied as he opened the case and removed a yellowed, rolled-up piece of parchment. "If you require more funds, there might be something else you can handle for me."

Thalasia tucked her payment into her purse, attached it to her belt loop, and strode over to a nearby case. "As intriguing as that sounds, I think it's time I depart this town."

"Oh?" Ayumu lifted the scroll above his head. A large, black-feathered owl swooped through the air and snatched the paper from his hand.

What the fuck? Where had that thing come from? She scanned the rafters. Where had it gone? A shiver shot down her spine and a sharp pain radiated from the base of her skull to the front of her head. *Shit!* Her mind opened as a vision flooded her brain.

The little Seelie girl stepped back. Her dirty, cinnamon-colored hair hung back over her shoulders, caked with mud. Her round, hazel eyes widened as she whimpered, "Please...don't hurt me."

Taking another step back, she tripped over a bloody limb torn from its body. The little girl shrieked and scrambled backward until she hit a nearby hut. She pressed her back against the wall, drew her legs close to her body, and pleaded, "Please...please, don't hurt me."

Tears trickled down the little girl's swollen cheeks. "Please," she cried. The distance between them closed. "No!" the girl screamed.

Gasping for air, Thalasia fell backward. As she landed on her butt, she bumped into the bookcase next to her and knocked over a crystal ball. It rolled a couple of feet and stopped. "No," she muttered. This wasn't happening. Except she couldn't deny what she'd just seen, though she refused to respond. The gods or goddesses...whoever sent them couldn't make her.

"Thalasia?" Ayumu's eyebrows furrowed.

Her gaze flicked from the shaman to the crystal ball. She caught her reflection in it. A pair of deep set, bright silver eyes and an ashen face stared back at her. Not again. She hadn't had a vision in months. They were supposed to be gone. They couldn't have returned. "No!" Thalasia clambered to her feet and ran as if her life depended on it. Maybe it wouldn't help her escape the vision, but maybe it would. The only way she'd find out was if she tried.

She flicked her wrist, unlocked and opened the door, and darted out of the store. Leaving it all in her wake, she rounded the corner and shot into the crowd. Her feet pounded against the pavement as she hoofed it as far away as she could get. She had to escape these visions.

They had already cost her too much.

There wasn't anything left for her to give.

Not even her heart.

Two

Thalasia glanced at the loud drunkards gathered at the bar from her corner booth. It seemed a little early for anyone to be so raucous, but as long as they didn't bother her, she didn't care. Instead, she focused on the remnants of her dinner as the earlier event replayed in her mind.

Rounding the corner, Thalasia skidded to a stop and bent over as she desperately tried to catch her breath. She crouched down, dug her elbows into her knees, and shoved her hands into her hair. They were gone. The visions were gone. Not one had popped up since... NO! She couldn't think about that. But no matter how hard she tried to keep it at bay, the memory danced across her brain like a forgotten lullaby.

"Run," Klaus ordered. "You need to run!"

"No! I can't! I won't leave you behind." She couldn't do this again. Leave another person, only to lose them. Because that's what would happen. She could feel it in her bones. Mistress was coming and he couldn't fight alone.

"You must." He removed something from the pocket of his pants and tucked the cool, glowing metal into her palm. "Take this. As long as you have it, I can find you. But you must go, Thalasia. You're the future. Now go! Fly to the jump-point and don't look back."

Clutching the radiant token tight in her hand, she threw her arms around him. "Thank you. For everything." He'd gotten her out of there, saved her life. And he was doing it again. Releasing the hug, she nodded once to him and took off into the air. Once again, leaving someone she cared about behind.

Tears pricked the corners of her eyes. With the back of her knuckles, Thalasia quickly brushed them off. This wasn't the time or place for crying.

"You okay?" the server asked as she poured more water into the cup.

"I'm fine," Thalasia declared. Her wellbeing didn't concern the woman. "Just get me the check."

"You don't look it, but I go with what you say." The server set a piece of parchment down with some numbers scribbled on it. "I come back."

Despite the female's thick accent, she understood all of it. At least until the server hollered something at the barkeep. Gods, she should've learned some of the language here. Thalasia eyed the total amount due on the paper. Another thing she should've figured out by now. How to convert their monetary values to gold. Lifting the cup to her lips, she took a big gulp of water and dug into her purse. She laid five gold coins on the table, rose to her feet, and headed for the door.

It was time to blow this realm. Not that she knew where to go next. Maybe if she consulted the book...no, that could be dangerous. She'd already had one vision, it could easily trigger another. Thalasia exited the building and stepped into a back alley. The stench of day-old garbage tickled her nose. Nothing like the pungent smell of urine to wake up the senses. But she'd take it over the sweet scent of bread or fruit. In the human world, anyway. Places like this dive didn't ask questions.

Of all the species she'd ever encountered, humans were the nosiest. Though it was easier to blend in with them. She only had to glamour her wings. Thalasia shoved her hands in the pockets of her jeans and strolled toward the street ahead. As much as she wanted to find an inn for the night, the forest might offer her better protection. And she'd be close to the jump-point.

Behind her, a door creaked open and shut. She glanced over her shoulder and noticed a group of young men leave the restaurant. They started in her direction, and a chill shot down her spine. No reason for her to read anything into it. People often left places and walked the same path as others. It didn't mean they were following her, even if they were the drunkards she'd seen at dinner.

Shaking the sensation off, she focused on where she was going but kept her senses heightened. Best to be prepared. Just in case, she picked up her pace.

Their steps echoed against the pavement as the three males walked faster. "Hey, girl," one called out. "Where are your parents?"

"Not safe for someone so young to be out here alone," another stated.

Shit. They were following her. How the fuck was she going to get out of this? Maybe if she pretended they weren't there, then they'd go away. Ignoring them, she huddled in her leather jacket a little more and increased her pace again.

One male jogged and caught up with her. He grabbed her arm and yanked her back a bit. "See, it's not safe."

Thalasia dug her heel in and adjusted her stance. The guy had moved her once. It wouldn't happen again. Especially as the other two trailed behind him, taking up space on either side of her. The three of them boxed her in. All right. If they wanted a fight, she'd give them one. She balled up her fists and narrowed her eyes at the males. "I'm fully capable of protecting myself," she spat. "So you have one last chance to walk away."

One of them snickered. "Three against one, little girl," he said as he closed the distance between them. "But maybe if you give us some of that gold, then we'll let you go."

She'd itched for a good fight all day. And this guy just gave her the perfect reason to start one. He had at least half a foot on her, but in her world, that didn't mean shit. She stomped on his foot and threw a right hook, sending him stumbling backward. The other two lunged at her simultaneously. Thalasia ducked a punch, elbowed one in the gut, and struck the other in the chest. Although it knocked them both back, the fight wasn't over yet.

The first male she'd hit kicked the back of her thigh, driving her down to one knee. The sting shot down her leg. As her eyes widened, showing the whites, her hands clenched. This fucker had a lot of nerve attacking her. Dropping low, she dodged the sidekick that came at her and drew the blade she kept tucked underneath her belt. With a guttural roar, she drove it hard into his thigh and ripped it free. He shrieked as blood splattered all over her face.

"Please," the Seelie girl pleaded as she tripped over a partially shredded limb, crimson staining the ground beneath it. "Please, don't hurt me."

A twinge shot up the back of Thalasia's skull. "No," she groaned. Trying to shake off the vision, she struggled to her feet and staggered backward. The blade fell from her hand and skittered across the pavement.

Red grime matted the girl's brown hair beneath a golden crown. The Seelie pressed her back against a hut, slid down to the dirt floor, and drew her knees to her chest. She lifted her hazel eyes. "Please," she begged. "Let me go."

"Bitch!" a male hollered as his fist connected with Thalasia's face.

A slight crunch rang out in her ears as blood gushed from her nose. It only intensified the throbbing in her head, almost like a battering ram repeatedly slamming against her brain.

"No!" the Seelie girl screamed.

Someone's foot hit her square in the chest and sent her flying backward. Thalasia slammed into a brick wall. With an agonizing grunt, she dropped to her knees.

A bloody hand reached toward the young Seelie. Tears pricked the corners of her eyes as she shrieked.

Thalasia pressed the heel of her palm against one eye. Not that it staved off the pain radiating across her mind. Even the completion of her vision didn't help.

One attacker shoved her back and reached for her purse. As her gaze lifted to the dark-haired male, her wings sprang forth. The male's brown eyes widened, his tan face turned pallid and his forehead beaded with sweat. "What the fuck?" he screeched.

Shit. She must've lost control of her glamour. Given the ache that had set up shop in her head, she didn't have the capacity to manipulate their minds. Which only left her with one option. Thalasia grabbed the guy's arm and sent a jolt of lightning through his body. As he landed on the ground, writhing in pain, she scrambled to her feet. She quickly located her dagger, picked it up, tucked it away, and ran.

It wouldn't take but a moment to reclaim her glamour, but she could do that and get away at the same time. She'd deal with her injuries later. Getting away was more important than anything else right now, though it seemed she couldn't escape her visions. At least if the agony rooted deep in her mind was anything to go by. This was worse than the one she had earlier.

The gods weren't giving her a choice this time. Not only did she have to leave the human world, she had to go where they wanted. Or face the consequences.

Thalasia drank in the large temple standing before her. Stone lanterns lined the staircase leading to the entryway. The shrine stood three stories tall, each part with a red roof inlaid with intricate gold designs. The gold continued underneath each level of the pavilion.

It shone brilliantly beneath the sunlight, casting exquisitely on the plunge pool behind it. Especially as the waterfall cascaded down, spraying into the pool at the bottom. The roar of the water brought a smile to her face. Although the shrine was to some dragon, she could stand there all day basking in its glory. It didn't matter that she'd come through it once already, it would always take her breath away.

Gods, she'd miss this, but she had a job to do. Thalasia smirked. Something she never thought she'd think about again, but she didn't have a choice. Letting out a heavy sigh, she ascended the staircase and entered the temple. As she crossed the threshold, she surveyed her surroundings. Thankfully, the place appeared empty. It was too early in the day for purveyors and worshippers, though she'd still have to watch out for those who maintained the grounds.

Her gaze flicked to the two dragon statues sitting on either side of a set of bamboo doors that led to the main hall. From what little she'd gathered, it was one area open to the public. Silence greeted her, which meant it was completely empty. Thalasia strode forward, quietly slipped through the doors, and stepped around the corner to the hidden second-level entrance. The jump-point itself was in the temple's third story.

This was where things got fun. Hopefully, she wouldn't run into any priests or priestesses this time around. At least she'd gotten them to forget all about her arrival. Getting them to forget about her departure might be harder unless she knocked them out. Thalasia shrugged. It was certainly an option.

Gently, she shut the door behind her and took the spiraling staircase two steps at a time. The quicker she got there, the faster she could get out of here. She would've come last night, except she needed to do some digging about the realm she had to go to. Though she hadn't found much of anything regarding Trozenia. It wasn't somewhere her predecessors had traveled. All she had to go on was the short list of known species: humans, elves, and minotaurs.

Thalasia hit the landing of the second floor and paused briefly. She heightened her senses, listening carefully for voices on the other side. Still nothing. She continued her ascent to the top floor. As she approached the top of the staircase, she used her glamour and altered her ears, the outer tip elongating into a point. She'd already hidden her wings, and dressed in a natural leather halter, skirt, and boots, so there wasn't anything else to change.

Or so she hoped.

Stopping at the third-floor landing, Thalasia stilled and shut her eyes. Droplets of water hit the rocks and leaves surrounding the sanctuary. All the sounds she heard came from outside the temple, but nothing from the prayer room itself. Good. Slowly, she turned the knob and slipped into the heart of the shrine.

A golden statue of an enormous dragon with sapphire blue eyes sat in the middle of the room. Depictions of a great battle covered the walls, but she didn't understand any part of the story beyond that. Quietly, Thalasia closed the door and crossed the room. Standing in front of the statue, she stared at it. The piece was twice her height and size. "No way this is accurate," she mumbled.

Dragons were much larger than this bust portrayed.

Shaking the thought from her head, Thalasia focused on the symbols she needed to draw. Adjusting the gold chain around her neck, she removed the lyre charm from beneath her halter and stroked her forefinger across its strings. A silver glow coated her hand.

The air rippled as she lifted her fingers and carefully painted each mark in the air. One wrong line or misplaced symbol, and she'd end up somewhere other than where she intended. Thalasia got the last piece set. Just as the jump-point opened, the side door cracked open, and a priest entered the room. "Shit," she muttered.

He screamed something at her in a foreign language, though she imagined it was along the lines of, *"Who are you? What are you doing here? You don't belong here!"*

Either way, she couldn't have him blabbing to his friends that he'd seen her. Thalasia eyed the jump-point out of her periphery as it pulsated. "Sorry about this," she stated to the bald male. She opened her mouth and let out a low aria. He went silent and stood completely motionless. Lifting her voice higher, she manipulated his memories and wiped the last sixty seconds from his synapses. Without releasing the note, Thalasia slowly backed up and stepped through the jump-point.

The dragon statue behind her disappeared from her sight. Bright hues of blue and purple swirled around her as the portal engulfed her. A multitude of colors raced past her as she walked forward. It was like a rainbow swallowed her and spit her out into a new world. She exited the jump-point, stepping onto a dirt road surrounded by an endless sea of lush green trees. A group of humans brandishing swords encircled her. *Crap.* She'd stepped out of a small fire and waltzed right into a burning blaze.

There were too many for her to use her siren song like she'd done with the priest mere moments ago. Maybe they wouldn't—one of them swung their blade at her. Thalasia jumped back, barely dodging the hit. "Guess that answers that question." She drew her dagger from her skirt's hidden pocket. While she'd do whatever it took to protect herself, it was wise to keep the extent of her powers hidden.

She evaded most of their strikes. The blade's sharp edge sliced her arm, which was better than the alternative. They'd come awfully close to hitting her in the belly. Going on the offensive, Thalasia faked a parried step to the left and threw her dagger. She hit the man in the neck. Blood gushed out from his throat as he grabbed at it and fell to his knees. Before any of the others could come at her, she spun on the back of her heel and threw a bolt of lightning at the next closest person.

A loud *thunk* rang out. Her gaze snapped toward one of the four remaining humans. Well, three...an arrow whizzed by her face as another *thunk* resounded not a foot in front of her. Thalasia's head swiveled toward the noise just as the male dropped his sword. It skittered across the dirt floor. If he'd gotten any closer...her eyes widened as she swallowed to wet her parched throat. She didn't know who, but someone had just saved her life.

Not that she could think about that right this second. Two humans remained. Thalasia focused on them. A brown-skinned elf landed on the ground with ease. Before the humans could react, the female thrust her spear into the belly of one and then the other. They both flopped limply to the ground, crimson pooling beneath each of their bodies and staining the land red.

An elf with long, caramel-colored hair touched down beside the other female. They glanced at one another. "You are who?" the brown-skinned one asked in Elvish.

No elf she'd ever crossed paths with in the past had organized their words like that. Although she understood what the female said, the dialect was strange. It wasn't something she could match, but she would do what she could. "My name is Thalasia," she replied in Elvish as she crossed over to the human she'd killed and yanked out her dagger.

"You came from where?"

Oh, how to answer that? Atlis rules forbade her from disclosing the truth of her...inheritance and purpose. But it might make things go faster if she could offer them something. Maybe a half-truth. Or the truth without details. She wiped the blood from her blade on the human's clothes and sheathed it back in its hiding spot. "I'm a world traveler." Thalasia flicked her gaze from one female to the other. "Who are you?"

The brown-skinned female's mouth pinched as she lowered her chin, looking down on Thalasia. "The ones who saved your life."

"I am called Camylla," the other female answered. "And she is called Rylln."

"Cam!" Rylln growled. "You should not tell her that. We owe her nothing."

"She has answered our questions without resistance. It is of little consequence to give her our names. Just polite," Camylla stated. Brushing her caramel-colored hair over her shoulder, she focused her green eyes on Thalasia. "You are alone?"

"Yes." That much was obvious. It wasn't as if anyone else was around. With that question, the conversation could only go in one direction. She had to head it off before it got too far. "I'm an orphan."

Camylla retrieved her arrows from the two dead bodies and placed them in the quiver slung across her back. "We need to handle this."

"Agreed," Rylln grunted. Her brown eyes narrowed at Thalasia. "What do we do with her?"

"Take her with us."

"No! Absolutely not."

"You heard her, Ry. She has no one. With what she did, she could be of use," Camylla claimed. "A decision that only Arel can make."

"Fine." Grumbling under her breath, Rylln flicked her wrist and all six bodies levitated. She muttered something and the dead humans floated through the air, deeper into the forest.

Thalasia cocked an eyebrow and tilted her head. She watched as the corpses disappeared. Her ears prickled as the bodies dropped somewhere in the forest. A fire sprang to life. "What are you doing with them?"

"Destroying them. If they are discovered, it will start a war," Camylla replied. "Humans dislike us." She inhaled a deep breath and blew it out. Sand swirled in the air, covering the mess created on the dirt floor.

"No one likes us," Rylln tacked on.

Great, Thalasia thought to herself. Of all the species she could've disguised herself as she had to choose a hated one. Well, that certainly wasn't going to make things easier. Not that she could change it now. Though it certainly explained her vision. And why the humans attacked her without provocation. "If that's true, then it sounds to me like you're already at war."

"Smart girl." Camylla cracked a slight grin at her. "Now come. We must go."

Right. To see this Arel person, whoever that was... Gods, she wished she'd never come here. Thalasia peered at the jump-point. It would take too long to initiate it, even if she had an idea of where to go. Which meant she'd have to kill the two females that just saved her life. That made less sense than seeing where the path led her. If she only lived a few more days, at least she'd get to see her family again. Shaking off the thought, she started forward and trailed behind Camylla and Rylln.

The past had to stay buried. Otherwise, she'd never do what she came to do. Survive.

Three

Thalasia surveyed her surroundings as they trekked through the tallest trees she'd ever seen before. It was almost as if the fae village brushed the sky. She clung to the rope banister as they crossed a wooden bridge, leading them from one tree to the next. The bridge groaned slightly as it swayed beneath her feet. She peered over the side, hesitating for a moment. It was a long fall to the bottom. Although she had wings, she couldn't reveal the truth of her existence to these people. It was the number one rule Demeter gave the first Atlis upon their creation. At least according to the way her mother told it.

"Your powers come from many gods and goddesses, Thalasia."

"What do you mean, Mama?" she asked. *That didn't make any sense. Why did that matter in keeping their existence a secret?*

"Well, I told you how Demeter created us, right?"

"Yes. After she lost her daughter, she gave Persephone's nymph friend's wings so they could find her, but they couldn't. Then she found out from someone else who stole her, so she made the Atlis because she didn't want any mother to suffer like her." It wasn't word-for-word, but it was the story her mama had told her many times before.

"Right. And she got a lot of gifts from the other gods and goddesses. Like Aphrodite, who granted us with beauty; Athena, who gifted us with wisdom; Ares, who gave us skill in combat; Apollo, who granted us with the power of sight; Hermes, who granted us with song; Poseidon, who gifted us with power

over the sea; and Zeus, who gave us control of lightning and air. These are all secrets we must protect. People can believe that we're a myth only, otherwise, we'll never be able to complete our missions properly. Do you understand?"

"Yes, Mama."

Yeah. The mission always took priority over anything else, including their lives. Thalasia shook the memory off, burying it down deep. She couldn't think about her mother right now. Not even an auspicious moment like that one. It only ever ended one way—in tears.

No one here needed to see her scars, emotional or physical. She rolled her shoulders, releasing the tension that had crept into her body as they crossed another bridge. Thalasia narrowed her eyes at the group of elves dressed in leather armor gathered in front of a silver-haired male. She flicked her gaze to Camylla as the female slowed her pace. Camylla exchanged a glance with Rylln, who trailed behind Thalasia. "Is this normal?" Thalasia asked.

"No," Camylla replied.

"Now, go!" the silver-haired male proclaimed. "Do not return until you find her!"

Could this be the village that the elf child she'd seen in her vision had disappeared from? If so, the collection of warriors made sense. Thalasia eyed the male out of her periphery. A single braid hung in front of one pointed ear as his ice-blue eyes focused on the crowd's dispersal. Several tattoos covered his chest and neck, but she couldn't quite make out the design. The dark blue duster he wore hid much of it. He shoved a hand through his hair, gripping it in his fist.

Was this Arel? Camylla continued forward, leading their small group toward him. And could it be his daughter that had gone missing? He acted like a concerned father. Maybe even an angry one. She needed confirmation before she offered aid, provided they would accept it.

"Arel," Camylla called out. "Tell me what has happened."

"They have taken Alyndra," he stated as he paced back and forth. "I do not..." his words trailed off. He halted in his steps, his eyes zeroing in on Thalasia. "Who is this? What is she doing here?"

"This is Thalasia," Rylln responded. "Cam thought her an orphan that we needed to bring with us."

Camylla narrowed her eyes at the female. "That is not the only reason," she snapped.

Arel stepped closer to Camylla. "Then why is *she* here?"

The female glimpsed at Thalasia. Camylla closed the distance between her and Arel. "I believe she is a walker."

What the hell was a walker? And why had the female spoken to Arel in a hushed tone? Did Camylla think she couldn't hear her? Elves had excellent hearing and sight. Although she wasn't actually an elf, both still applied. One of the many gifts given to the Atlis. Thalasia kept from rolling her eyes and focused instead on the exchange between Arel and Camylla.

"That is not possible. They do not exist."

"Arel, I swear to you...she *is* a walker. And a powerful one. She appeared out of nowhere and dispatched two humans with magic not seen before."

Damn. The entire trek here and she hadn't once considered that they'd arrived on that scene prior to her. Or that they'd witnessed her blip out of thin air. She'd never known an elf to have any kind of comprehension of how it was possible. Though it sounded like they had their own myths about it. Something that would've been great to know beforehand.

"Rylln, you are rather quiet. Do you not agree?" Arel asked.

"I think we have more questions than answers regarding the child."

Arel strode over to where Thalasia stood. As he clasped his hands at the small of his back, he scrutinized her slight form. "Are you a walker?"

"I can't answer that."

"It is a simple question."

"To you maybe, but to me it isn't." Thalasia interlaced her fingers. It was the only way to keep from folding her arms. While she didn't want to offend him, she also didn't want to appear defensive. "I don't know what a walker is, so I can't answer your question."

"Someone who can walk between worlds," Camylla replied.

Arel's eyebrows furrowed as he jerked his head in the female's direction. "It is not your job to share knowledge. Especially something she should have known as an elf."

No elves that she'd ever crossed paths with had used the term before. And it certainly didn't mean the same thing to her people, not that she could admit as much. "Yes, I'm a walker."

"Yet you are an orphan?" he questioned. Arel's face tightened and his lips pressed together into a thin line. He shook his head. "One is not possible if the other is true."

Thalasia dug her nails into her palm. It was bad enough that he called her a liar, but for him to think she'd lie about her parents... She clenched her jaw and drew in a slow, steady breath. "Believe it or not, that's your choice. It doesn't mean it isn't true." She met his gaze. "I'm here to offer my help. To get Alyndra back, who I'm presuming is your daughter."

His mouth downturned as his chin dropped. Arel scoffed and peered down his nose at her. "Whether it is true is irrelevant. You are a child. It would be unwise to risk the lives of my people and entrust a child, especially one I do not know." He glanced at Rylln. "Take her somewhere safe." Waving a hand dismissively, he spun on the back of his heel.

Heat flushed her body. She ground her teeth. Her jaw ached, but she refused to give into her desire to just beat the shit out of this arrogant male. Thalasia rolled her shoulders and folded her arms across her chest. It wouldn't do her a damn bit of good to fail at her mission. While she could certainly handle things on her own, she still had to confirm *who* she had to save. "Alyndra...she has brown hair, hazel eyes, and wears a golden crown with butterfly wings."

Arel narrowed his eyes at her. His nose wrinkled as if a foul scent had blown through. "It is impossible for you to know that. Unless..." His words trailed off as his entire body stiffened. "She is a traitor! Arrest her!"

"What are you—" A pair of silver cuffs snapped onto her wrists, cutting her question off. Thalasia glared at Rylln, who stood there with a smirk on her face. Well, shit. This wasn't what she had in mind for affirming her suspicions. *Good move,* she thought to herself. Now, what did she do?

"Take her away!" Arel ordered.

"As you wish," Rylln replied. She yanked on the chains, tugging Thalasia along. "Move."

The last thing she heard as Rylln dragged her off to only the gods knew where was an argument between Camylla and Arel. Unfortunately, their words came out so fast that she didn't quite catch everything. But one thing stuck out—minotaurs. Thalasia bit back a groan. Didn't this mission just get better and better? Just one more problem to add to the ever-growing list. She couldn't say what was worse: this or dealing with the humans.

Thalasia slammed her fist into the stone wall, but it didn't crack or even dent. "Shit." No matter how many ways she attempted to get out of this cell, she couldn't break any damn part of it. Not the metal bars or the lock. If she had her dagger, she could've used that to pick the lock, but that woman had stolen it.

This was what she got for listening to the damn gods! A whole shitload of problems. If she couldn't get out of this cell, then whatever the minotaurs did to that girl was on her hands. With a loud groan, she kicked the silver bars. They didn't even budge. Thalasia shoved a hand into her blue hair and gripped it hard. How the fuck was she supposed to get out of here?

She glimpsed the floating map out of her periphery. It had nearly finished collecting details about this realm—forests, mountains, towns, and so on. Thalasia eyed the barrier trapping her in this jail and gazed at the bands wrapped tightly around her wrists. She had no issue with her glamour, or accessing any of the magical items in the purse she'd hidden under her skirt. Though her earlier attempt at her siren song on the guards failed. The prison didn't prevent magic, only the cuffs impacted it. Thalasia chewed on the inside of her cheek. That didn't mean she couldn't escape.

She strode to where the map hung in the air and scanned the various territories. Just as she suspected, she'd found herself among wood elves. Another area belonged to silver elves, somewhere to the west. Humans lived to the east, minotaurs took up the south, and centaurs ran along the north. Certainly an interesting combination. As she watched the last few lines fill in on the map, she dug into her purple pouch. Her ancestors had collected a multitude of items over the centuries, and she was fairly positive the bag contained something that would help.

Searching through the various pockets, she monitored the map as it finished. There were so many damn things in here, but she was looking for one particular item. Where the fuck was it? Maybe down by the journals. Thalasia dug deeper into her purse. As much as she loved the extension charm, sometimes she despised—"Aha!" As she pulled a skeleton key out, she beamed. Oh, yes. This would do just perfectly.

Maybe. One way to find out. With the map completed, she rolled it up and tucked it away. No need to have it out yet. Thalasia crossed the cell, peered both ways down the hall, and hooked an arm around one bar. Remaining vigilant, she struggled to get the key into the right hole. It took longer than expected, but she succeeded. Slowly, she turned it toward the right and the door creaked ever so slightly.

Retrieving the key from the keyhole, Thalasia nudged the cell door open a little farther and slipped into the hallway. She pressed her back against the wall, closely monitoring both sides. While she'd tracked how they'd taken her to the prison, it wasn't the best way out. And she couldn't consult the map without taking a chance they'd catch her. Shit. Which direction did she go? "Pick one and pray," she muttered.

No. That wouldn't work. Thalasia peered one way down the corridor and then the other. Torches flickered, causing shadows to dance across the stone walls. When Rylln had dragged her down here, they'd descended beneath the trees. While their homes were closer to the sky, their prisons were under the earth. A slow grin crossed her face. It should be easy to find her way out. All she had to do was follow the thick scent of dank water. She sniffed the air. Left should lead her out. Or closer to the top.

Thalasia strode forward but kept her senses alert for even the slightest sound. The only way she'd successfully get out of here was if she didn't run into anyone. Glancing over her shoulder, she rounded the corner and slammed right into someone. *Shit.* Her gaze narrowed on the female standing in front of her.

Staring at her, Camylla smirked. "Follow me."

Okay. That wasn't what she expected. Maybe it wasn't the wisest choice to trust the female, but the woman had defended her several times. Besides, she didn't have any other choice. Thalasia dipped her chin and prayed to Demeter this wasn't the biggest mistake of her life.

"Are you going to tell me what's going on or am I just supposed to guess?" Thalasia questioned. Camylla had gotten her out of the labyrinth that was the Elven prison and away from their territory. Thankfully, they hadn't run into anyone else on their way out.

Camylla peered over her shoulder. She removed a dagger from her left side, flipped it in the air, caught it, and held it out to Thalasia by the hilt. "You may want this where we are going."

She canted her head at the female. That didn't exactly answer her question. At least she got her dagger back—the last gift she'd ever received from her father. Wrapping her fingers around the handle, the Atlis crest pressed warmly against her palm. Had Camylla noticed the wings that tightly gripped a sword with an intricately designed poppy flower in the hilt? Even if the female had, it wasn't a widely recognized emblem. Only another Atlis would know it. Or a sentry, but she hadn't seen one of them in years. And she was the only living Atlis. Thalasia sheathed the dagger in the back of her skirt. "Where are we going?"

"To rescue the princess."

"You mean we're going to where the minotaurs are," Thalasia corrected. Though both likely applied. If they found one, then they'd probably find the other. The female raised an eyebrow at her, but said nothing. She cocked one corner of her mouth and shrugged. "I didn't understand a lot of yours and Arel's argument, except that."

"I told him he was making a mistake by arresting you. That you were not in cahoots with the minotaurs and there was another reason you knew what Alyndra looked like. Despite all the reasons I provided, he refused to accept you as a walker."

"Yet you went against him and freed me anyway. Why?" An answer she desperately needed. She didn't trust easily. And she had to know whether she could trust Camylla. More than she already had.

The female let out an exasperated sigh and ran a hand down her peasant blouse. "Every year, at the time of the harvest, the minotaurs make a blood sacrifice to their god, Minos. This has gone on for centuries. In the beginning, they used to steal and enslave human children. Then they moved on to Elven children. Regardless of our efforts, we have never successfully made it through their labyrinth and stopped this from happening. I believe you might be our only hope of changing that."

Well, hell. That explained so much of her vision. The girl had to be backing away from a minotaur. Wait. No. That couldn't be right. She'd seen minotaur limbs scattered across the ground. Thalasia canted her head at Camylla. "That sounds like a colossal risk and a lot of faith to put in someone you don't know, let alone a child."

Camylla halted in her steps. "Perhaps, but I saw how you appeared out of nowhere and what you did to that human. The stench of his charred skin is burned into my memory. You are no ordinary child, regardless of what you declare."

"Point taken. Although some of that might be difficult as long as I still have these on." Thalasia lifted her arms and gestured to the silver bracelets.

The female narrowed her green eyes at Thalasia. "If I remove them, how can I trust you will not run off and leave me to handle the situation alone?"

She chewed on the inside of her cheek. As much as she had to trust Camylla, Camylla had to trust her. "Because you're right. I'm not an ordinary child. I'm so much more than that. Besides, we have the same goal."

"Yes, I suppose we do." Camylla removed a small, straight silver bar from beneath her bracer. She touched it to the underside of each cuff and they fell from Thalasia's arms.

Rubbing her wrists, Thalasia scrutinized Camylla's outfit. The female was better dressed for war than she was. Thalasia dug her purse out from under her skirt. "Before we go any farther, I need to get suited up." She didn't have much in the way of armor, but some protection was better than none.

Especially with what they were about to face.

Four

Thalasia stared at the full moon as it rose over the horizon, coloring the sky in various hues of blue and purple. Despite the night's beauty hovering above them, it was anything but where she and Camylla hid. Hooves thundered against the ground. She pressed up against a stone wall, blending into the darkness that bled down on them. Several minotaurs passed by their location. Even with the map's help, it had taken them far too long to find their way through the labyrinth. They had no time to waste. Otherwise, this would all be for nothing.

Her eyes widened as she caught sight of a minotaur. The first she'd ever seen. It was huge, standing nearly twelve feet tall. That didn't account for all the muscle. Its biceps bulged and its legs were almost as wide as her whole body. With its large hooves, it could easily crush her beneath its foot. Or spear her with the horns atop its head. And that was just one! Did they all look like that? Another one stopped beside the other minotaur. There wasn't much difference between them, except maybe a few inches in height.

Shit! How the fuck am I supposed to defeat these damn things? Even with her powers, it would be impossible. The gods had sent her on a mission that was doomed to fail. Was this punishment for the last year? For all the visions she'd ignored?

No. That couldn't be it. Demeter wouldn't risk a child's life like that. No self-respecting god or goddess would. Well...not all of them. There was

Nyx, but even that seemed like too much. Maybe she was just overthinking all of this. They didn't have the hide of a dragon. Killing these creatures wasn't impossible. Thalasia peered over her shoulder at her companion.

What had the female said about why they couldn't defeat the minotaurs? Right! The elves had never made it through the labyrinth. They had, which already got them closer to rescuing Alyndra, so their success was inevitable. She zeroed in on the two minotaurs, chit-chatting amongst themselves. "You take the smaller one. The bigger one is mine," Thalasia muttered. She crouched down on her haunches and slowly unsheathed her sword and dagger.

Camylla grabbed her arm. "No. We need to be stealthy and find the princess. We cannot win in a fight against them."

Thalasia froze, her feet rooting her to the ground at the cave's mouth. A shiver shot down her spine. Mistress was coming for her. No, she couldn't let that happen again. Tightening her shoulders, she lifted her chin and clenched her fists.

"You need to go," Klaus stated. "Before they get any closer."

"No. I can fight. I'm not leaving." She'd done that one too many times in her life. Running away never solved problems. It just left them there to fester.

He kneeled down and grabbed her arms. "You can't win in a fight against her. And I won't give that woman another chance to kidnap you. Do you understand me? You run."

"But I'm strong now! I'm trained to fight."

"No!" he barked. "Run, Thalasia! That's what you do."

One memory bled into another. *"I need you to fly, Thalasia." Her mother took her hands within her own and pressed a kiss to her knuckles. "Do you hear me?"*

"Why? Is something coming? If so, I can fight. You taught me to fight." That was her role, right? Part of her purpose? To fight the evil. No matter what form it came in.

"You can't fight them. Not this time, sweetheart." Her mother rose to her feet. "One day, perhaps, but right now, you need to fly."

"But, Mom, I don't want to leave you." Why wouldn't they let her fight? Whatever it was coming for them, they could defeat it together.

"I know." A soft, sad smile crossed her mother's face. "I need you to fly, Thalasia. As fast as you can to the nearest jump-point. You must leave and never look back."

They all wanted her to run. She always ran. Like a coward, she let someone else fight her battles, and it always ended horribly. Thalasia shrugged off Camylla's grip and glared at the female. "No. The last time I didn't fight, everyone died! Never again!" She dropped her glamour, freeing her wings from their confines. Shaking them out, she rose to her full height of five feet, charged toward the minotaurs, and leaped into the air. As she landed on the back of the larger creature, she drove the tip of her sword into its neck and summoned the strongest bolt of lightning she could conjure, striking the other one down.

Thalasia hopped down as both creatures dropped to the ground with a loud thud. Her feet hit the dirt floor with grace. Glancing over her shoulder, she took stock of the crowd of minotaurs that had gathered. A sneer crossed her face as she clenched the hilts of her blades in each hand. Letting out a guttural roar, she raced toward the hoard.

Things were about to get messy.

Thalasia's chest heaved with each ragged breath she took. As the head she'd just lopped off stopped, she scanned the terrain and assessed the damage. Ash rained down atop the limbs strewn everywhere and the remnants of the minotaur bodies stacked upon one another. A river of blood covered the earth. She didn't know how many minotaur lives she'd ripped apart. Fifty. A hundred. Or even how much Camylla had contributed. Not that it mattered. It was done. The battle was over and they'd won.

As her breathing settled, she strode forward and stepped over one body part or another. There wasn't a point in tracking it. She just had to find Alyndra amidst this mess. Thalasia glimpsed movement out of her periphery. She halted and spun around on the back of her heel, holding her sword at the ready.

"There is no need for that," Camylla stated. With the back of her hand, the female wiped a crimson stain from her cheek. "The entire village is dead."

Lowering her blade, Thalasia dipped her chin. "Good." Just as she expected. "Have you found Alyndra?"

"No. Not yet."

"Then let's split up. I'll go this way; you go that way." They'd find the little girl faster. Once Camylla nodded her agreement, the two of them parted ways. Based on her vision, she'd locate the princess somewhere near a stone hut. There were several of them, and she'd killed countless minotaurs all over the place. It could take longer than necessary to scour through it all. Unless... Thalasia stopped in her tracks. She closed her eyes and heightened her other senses, listening for a sound that didn't belong and sniffing for something other than the copper scent that lingered in the air.

The sound of another's breaths bursting in and out and a racing heartbeat rang in her ears. Thalasia opened her eyes and followed the noise's origin. She circumvented a pile of bodies, climbed over some debris, and located the young princess near a couple of minotaur carcasses. "Alyndra?"

The elf girl's hazel eyes lifted to Thalasia. "Please," the girl pleaded as she backed up, tripping over a partially shredded limb, crimson staining the ground beneath it. "Please, don't hurt me."

What? Why would the female assume she was there to harm her? Maybe the little girl was confused. Or maybe this wasn't Alyndra? Thalasia took a step closer. "I'm not here to hurt you."

The little girl's eyes widened, and she blanched. Moving backward, the young elf pressed her back against a hut, slid down to the dirt floor, and drew her knees to her chest. "Please," she begged. "Let me go."

Why did it seem like this girl didn't believe her? Unless this really wasn't Alyndra. Had she gotten things wrong? Thalasia chewed on the inside of her cheek and scrutinized the young elf. Big hazel eyes. Red grime matted the girl's brown hair beneath a golden crown with butterflies at the edges. No. Everything she saw before her was in her vision. This had to be Alyndra. "I promise. I'm not going to hurt you." Her grip tightened on the hilts she held. Thalasia dropped her gaze to the two blades in her hands. That probably didn't help her cause. "I'm putting these up. Okay?" She returned her sword and dagger to their sheaths. "See?"

Alyndra shook her head. "Please," she mumbled. "I just want to go home." Tears rolled down the female's face.

"That's what I'll do. I'll take you home...back to your father." Thalasia held out a hand to the girl. "Come with me and you'll go home."

"No!" the elf child shrieked.

"Alyndra!" Camylla yelled as she raced past Thalasia. The woman skidded to a halt, crouched down on her haunches, and tightly embraced the elf child.

Thalasia stared at them both. It didn't make sense. Why wouldn't Alyndra take her hand? A drop of blood fell from her fingers and hit a small puddle. Lowering her arm, Thalasia glimpsed her reflection in the water.

Crimson streaked across her forehead, nose, and cheeks. It had also gotten caked in her wings, darkening their natural shade of blue. None of which included the blood that covered the rest of her body. Thalasia drank in the surrounding scene. Images of wings staked to the ground flashed in her mind. Memories of people tied up, pleading for their lives.

Wherever she went, death followed her. How many lives had she ripped apart? How many had sacrificed themselves so she could survive? All so she could become...*this*. She fell to her knees as tears pricked the corners of her eyes. All this time, she believed her vision showed Alyndra cowering from a monster. Just not the one she thought. "I'm the monster."

A droplet of rain hit her head. She lifted her gaze toward the sky as it opened up. It was almost as if the gods cried with her. As if they'd suffered alongside her this whole time. Shared in all the rage she'd carried over the loss of every person she'd ever loved. The rain trickled down her face, arms, and body, washing away the blood as if the brutality she'd unleashed never happened.

"You are no monster, Thalasia," Camylla declared. "The princess is safe because of you. As are many children. We will no longer fear what the harvest may bring."

Thalasia lowered her head, dropping her eyes to the ground. "That doesn't mean they all deserved what I delivered." Were there minotaurs she could've spared? Young that could've had a different future? It wasn't her place to be judge and executioner, yet that's what she'd done. One blow after another without pause over their differences; she'd killed an entire species. Why?

"Perhaps, but you did what was necessary. Sometimes that is not an easy action to take," Camylla said. "You carry a great weight. I may not know much about you, but I can see that. Do not feel you must understand everything all at once. Answers come when they are least expected."

"Thank you." A small hand caressed her cheek. "Pretty friend."

No one had ever called her a friend. It seemed like such a slight gesture. This young elf girl who cowered from her mere moments ago hadn't just touched her, but called her a friend. As she regarded the Elven child, the corners of her mouth upturned.

"Yes, a friend." Thalasia brushed the combined tears and rain from her face as she stood. She shifted her attention to Camylla. "Take her home. I'll handle...all this." She gestured to the mess.

"Thank you." Camylla took Alyndra's hand within her own. The two strode off and disappeared from Thalasia's sight.

The rain eased to a slight drizzle as Thalasia faced the carnage. It was a gruesome scene, but it wasn't something she ever wished to forget. Her anger had led her down this path, and it wasn't a place she could return. She'd set fire to it all and let her grievances burn with it. A strong enough blaze could consume the pain she'd tried so hard to forget.

Maybe that's what all of this had been about. Not just a reminder of her purpose, but that there was no way to let go of the past without facing it. Something she'd never done.

This was her second chance. An opportunity to do right by those who'd given their lives so she could continue forward. She couldn't do that if she ignored her visions. They were a part of her just as much as her parents and Klaus. It was time she did right by them and all of those she hadn't saved. That's what she'd do. One day at a time, until her last breath, she'd fight for those who couldn't fight for themselves. Because everyone needed a friend.

To Be Continued

In

Hunted

The Atlis Chronicles

Book One

About the author

ABOUT THE AUTHOR

Krys Fenner, also known as **Brigit Rosé**—like the wine, not the flower—has been infinitely passionate about writing and helping people for as long as she can remember. Having already published nine books, she avidly works on multiple series, from social issues to paranormal romance. While she loves everything she writes, she's genuinely excited about the other series she'll co-authors over the coming year. Krys received an Associate of Arts in Psychology, a Bachelor of Arts in Creative Writing, and is currently working on a Master's degree. When she isn't writing, she's spending time with her three fur babies, Bones, Luna, and Lola. To learn more about Krys Fenner and her upcoming book releases, visit her official website: https://kbfennerrose.com.

Also by Krys Fenner

ALSO BY KRYS FENNER
Dark Road Series
Addicted
Damaged
Avenged
Burned
Twisted
The Guardhian Series
Awakened
Disillusioned

Also by Brigit Rosé

ALSO BY BRIGIT ROSÉ
Love's Worth Series
UnHinged
ReIgnited
The Mystic Chronicles
Detached
The Lucent Chronicles
Grace's Beast
Shattered Wonderland
The Arcarean Academy
Wicked Ground

Co-Authored

CO-AUTHORED
Prisma Isle Series
Perfectly Reckless
Chaotic Tranquility
Rebel Tides

Coming Soon

COMING SOON
Betrayed (Dark Road Series)
ReUnited (Love's Worth Series)
Inherited (The Guardhian Series)
Siren's Curse (Prisma Isle Series)
Silencing the Shape Shifter (Prisma Isle Series)
Kingdom of Embers (Prisma Isle Series)
Hunted (The Atlis Chronicles)
Savage Ground (The Arcarean Academy)
Consumed (The Mystic Chronicles)
Dark Entanglement (The Midnight Chronicles)

www.ingramcontent.com/pod-product-compliance
Lightning Source LLC
Chambersburg PA
CBHW050441200726
48295CB00024B/935